The
Best Mom

For all the best moms, including my own – Dotti and Tri.
(And for Rebecca, of course, who really is amazing.) – P H

To Neve and Alex, always – S D

American edition published in 2021
by New Frontier Publishing Europe Ltd
www.newfrontierpublishing.us

First published in the UK in 2021
by New Frontier Publishing Europe Ltd
Uncommon, 126 New King's Road, London SW6 4LZ, United Kingdom
www.newfrontierpublishing.co.uk

ISBN: 978-1-913639-41-9

Distributed in the United States and Canada by Lerner Publishing Group Inc.
241 First Avenue North, Minneapolis, MN 55401 USA
www.lernerbooks.com

Library of Congress Cataloging-in-Publication data is available.

Designed by Verity Clark

Printed in China
1 3 5 7 9 10 8 6 4 2

The Best Mom

PENNY HARRISON SHARON DAVEY

NEW FRONTIER PUBLISHING

My friends have the BEST moms.
I'm hoping I might trade.
They're *never* late for anything.
They know each kind of braid.

Katie's moms are wizards
At dress-up days for school.

They snip and sew into the night,
With feathers, lace, and tulle.

My mom makes
my costumes

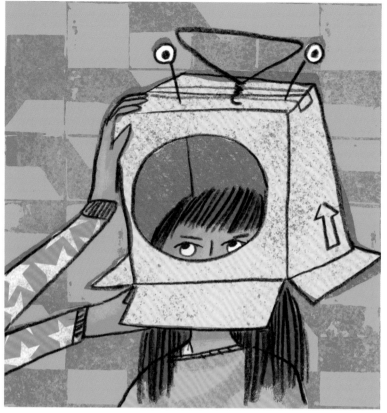

With sticky tape

and glue.

She **grunts** and **mutters** to herself,

Scout's mom is amazing.

She even roller skates.

She can swish and glide, just like a swan,

Into a **figure** eight.

My mom tried to **skate** once.
She was like a baby deer.

She

wibble-wobbled

on her feet

While everyone kept clear.

Jai's mom is a **pop** star.

She always sings along.

She **disco-dances**
on a chair
To every latest song.

My mom likes the opera.
She says it keeps her calm.

But when she tries to sing along,
It's like our car alarm.

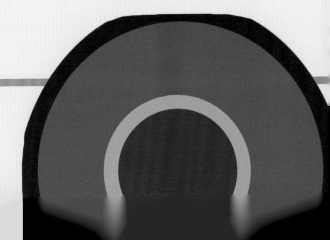

Eve's mom is a fairy.

I've even seen her wings.

She flutters through the playground

In her sparkly skirts and rings.

My mom doesn't flutter.

She *scrambles* out the gate.

Her shirt is always **inside** out,

Quick!

We're *always* running late.

Will's mom is a **top chef**
When cooking snacks and treats.

She makes sushi for his lunch box,
And rare, **exotic** sweets.

And when I open up my lunch
There's *always* something icky.

Huy's mom is an athlete.
She stretches at first light.

She **hikes** and **bikes** at weekends
And meditates each night.

My mom likes to sleep in.

When she runs, she gets a stitch.

And if she tries to meditate
Her left eye starts to twitch.

My friends have the best moms.
But mine will do just fine. . .

Cos when she **cuddles** me each night
I'm kind of glad she's mine.